3

by Sara Lippmann

Cover illustration: Alex Eben Meyer
Book design: Joe Lops

Addington CF and LTC Bodoni typefaces
provided by The Type Founders
thetypefounders.com

979-8-9918334-6-2

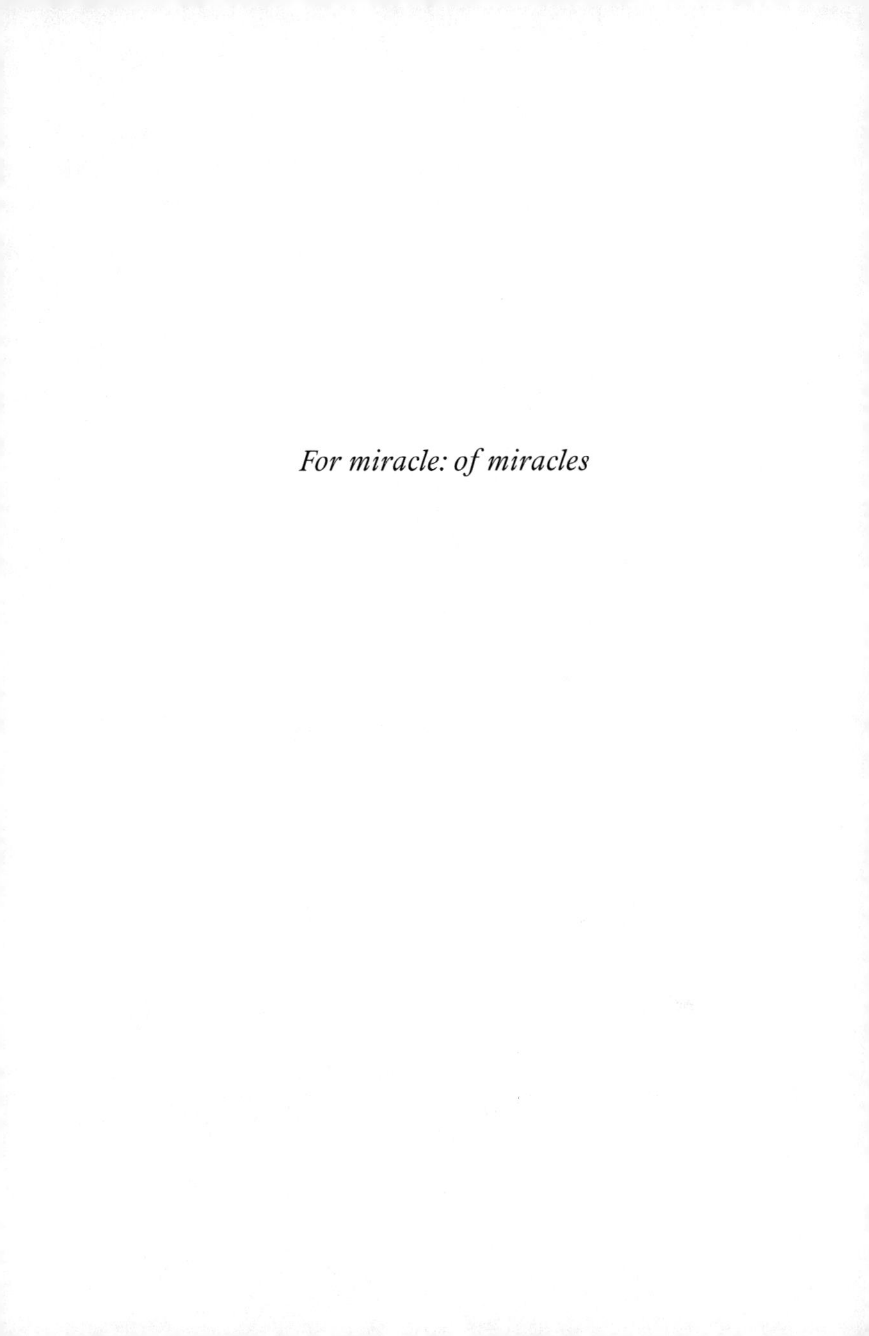

For miracle: of miracles

CONTENTS

LOOK YOURSELF

SHE MET THE PHOTOGRAPHER AT HER sister's wedding. It was a hell of a job, lining up a fleet of coiffed bridesmaids in ascending height, in eggshell sateen, in 105-degree heat. Her grandparents—soon to be dead—nearly croaked right then and there in the English garden among the giant alliums and Culver's root. The heat made guests so thirsty and therefore so drunk that people were making out against every gnarled, ancient tree, as if the whole wedding (minus those puking in a lilac bush) had been struck by Cupid's bow. It was a scene. Her sister was in love. She was alone, standing inside the steamy greenhouse looking out on the lawn when the photographer came upon her.

"Don't move," he said. "Right there. You're perfect. Just as you are." Before she could do anything, the camera clicked.

"I love how you're veiled by shadow *and* light." He inched closer, lens raised, like she was a gazelle he'd spotted from a distance on Jeep safari. She turned her head. Click. Lately, it had become nearly impossible for her to look anyone in the eye or hold a direct glance without breaking away and reflexively reaching for her face, her hair, her lips, but as he held her wrists—her pulse in his touch—and moved them off her body, click click click, there was no hiding, no ducking for cover. Color bloomed in her face, only this color was not from shame or unease. She, at 25, had come alive. He wore a leather harness like a foreign correspondent. He was around her age, or older. There was an agelessness about him, as if he'd always simply been around.

"How many rolls do you take?"

"As many as they pay me," he said, switching out canisters. Good, old-fashioned cellulose was still being used on the night that they met. She remembered taking a photography elective in high school. The marsupial smocks with the specially designed sleeves they wore for safe film removal and to prevent ruinous exposure, the piercing chemical scent of the developing baths. The claustrophobia of that coat closet cum dark room.

"Do you develop your own?"

"Yes," he said. "No. I mean, I *do*. With my *own* work. This is just a side gig. Weddings, anniversaries. Milestones are bread and butter. Really, I do editorial." With that he reached into his pocket and gave her his business card.

When she took him in again, not just his face,

but his entire carriage, his narrow build, she realized that she'd seen him before, his portfolio braced awkwardly under his arm. She worked the front desk at a popular fashion magazine. She manned reception. She wore skirts. She said things like "the editor will see you now." She escorted freelance hopefuls down the long, framed hallway to the art department. There was a steady stream of talent coming through: aspirational, nervous, deflated. Afterward, she pushed the button by the elevator bank to carry them down, saving them the embarrassment of trying to free up their hands. She said "have a nice day." Now looking at him—dusty hair longish by the ears, bushy at the sides, like he wanted a style but couldn't quite commit to one, more hippie than hipster—she was positive he'd made a cold pitch call. Maybe she'd glanced up from the stack of magazines she mindlessly flipped through all day long and seen him. Her only job was to look busy. Approachable yet unapproachable. The pay was shit, but one of the perks was a complimentary stack of every magazine that the publishing behemoth put out each month: 29 titles at its peak, excessive, even for a luxury brand. Who, besides her, could sit around reading all of them? No wonder the company would dissolve within the decade. The trees wasted alone.

She parted her lips as if to say something.

"This is just paying the bills," he said. "It's important to have aspiration."

Was shooting designer watches aspirational? Capturing windblown models on a hazardous cliff? What was her aspiration? He cupped her chin like a collectible figurine.

"Look at me," he said. She looked. He made her feel pretty, not sweaty or disheveled, not hopelessly plain, less lonely than she'd ever been. Did he recognize her too? Had she said "better luck next time?" Had they exchanged anything at all?

"To be clear," he went on. "Photography is my *passion*. And passion of any sort is an art. It's all about following that insatiable curiosity. Going deep on a subject, getting up-close, then closer still, seeing beyond what the naked eye can see."

For some reason, she thought of Oedipus Rex.

"Like an oracle?"

He chuckled. "I hate to brag—"

"There you are," a voice said, interrupting them. They turned. Down the hall a tall man in a dark suit—his hair a slick, silver wave—approached. His shoes tapped against the floor, a chunky heel, they were lifts. He said, "I can't have you going rogue, kid. I need you to carry my light."

• • •

WHEN IT WAS HER TURN to get married a few years later, it made sense that she'd look him up. She'd kept the card. His name was Norman Wax, an old man's name. He was still working for the same established wedding photographer, which elated her and also made her sad. On the website, he'd graduated from being a non-entity to having his own landing page complete with his own bio and head shot. She could hire him directly at an apprentice rate.

She and her fiancé went to meet him at an office on the west side. The space, above a wholesale fabric store, was barren and white, unfinished and austere, not what she'd expected. They sat in the waiting room on a black leather couch flipping through books.

Norman walked in and sank into the cushions beside her. Leather exhaled. The heat off his shoulder warmed her shoulder. They did not touch. He said, "Do you know what you're looking for?"

"An engagement photo."

He sucked his teeth. He could barely hide his disdain for *The New York Times*-style engagement-photo format, all those couples with their heads pressed together like conjoined twins. He'd rather capture people in their "natural habitat," he said, and because the studio, cut from a drafty warehouse of undergarment designers and shared workspaces, was hardly natural, down the industrial-grade elevator they went, and outside into the cold to frame the shot against a vibrant splash of graffiti between a dollar pizza shop and a dingy bodega.

"Much better," he said. They stood stiffly before the wall as if posing for mugshots, hesitant to press their backs against it. Face each other, the photographer commanded. She could feel Norman's eyes on her. People bustled by. Don't mind them. Everyone wants a glimpse of conjugal bliss. The photographer positioned their hands on their shoulders like middle schoolers at a dance. Picture your life together! Her eyes welled. Now, kiss! I feel like a buffoon, her fiancé almost said. The word baboon flew out instead. They laughed. Emotion! Her photographer clicked.

Ultimately, she hired the main guy, not his up-and-coming apprentice. The same photographer as her sister. The best in the business. No hard feelings, Norman said. Most people in this world stick with what they know.

• • •

On her wedding day, Norman showed up in the bridal suite anyway. Secretly, she'd hoped for this outcome. He was still an assistant, after all, and big festive affairs warranted multiple assistants. The deluxe photo package promised to capture—immortalize!—all stages of the magical day, so someone had to be there as she perched on the leopard skin pouf before the vanity in her girdle and strapless bra, as she slipped bobby pins into her tightly fastened chignon, as she leaned over the bulb-studded mirror to brighten the nervous pallor of her mouth. Forget about me, he said. I'm a fly on the wall. Later, there would be grainy shots of the slope of her neck, the arch of her spine. His wedding gift to her: casting her always in the best light. He tucked the wisps by her face, straightened her shoulders for a clean view of the pearl buttons running down the back of her dress, like she was some pristine package that had yet to be opened. She, who had never been photogenic, felt almost seductive before his lens. The proboscis of his Nikon tracing her slightest move.

She wished they could stay in the dressing room forever. Later, when the album arrived, these would be the images she'd love the most.

By the time the veil was secured by the teeth of a tortoise shell comb, he'd been replaced. Assistants were interchangeable and Norman had another gig to cover. He'd started booking his own affairs by now. Some chick with a buzz cut and a fitted tux stepped in. The female assistant wore a leather harness too. Like a dominatrix. Straight out of a sex den. The bride blushed beneath the huppah. Her eyes flitted over to the groom, his cummerbund ready to burst. Did they share the same thought? The world's shortest distance is between laughter and crying. No one zoomed in on her tears in black and white.

Work threw her a baby shower. Maybe they knew she wasn't coming back. Or maybe, more accurately, there would no longer be a job for her after the birth. What good was a mommy gal Friday? The engagement, the marriage, the pregnancy: it all happened in such rapid succession, at the overachieving clip of the city where everything—even love—was a competition. She was on the up and up.

Now she was in Norman's studio with a bump the size of a strap-on buoy.

"Look at you," he said, clapping his hands.

She reddened. It wasn't her idea, she preempted, already apologizing. Her colleagues had given her the portrait sit as a present to commemorate this life event, the momentous before and after—glossed body and all. Ever since that Demi Moore cover, all the women were doing it.

"Anyway," she said. "How have you been?"

"Good," he said. "Busy." Norman was milking the trend. Wink. Pun intended.

He led her to the back. He had rented the office next door to the main photographer.

Smaller, but at least it was his own. He was on his own now.

"Gotta stay hungry," he said. "Still working at the mothership?"

"Stop by sometime," she said, knowing by then she'd be gone.

She stripped down in a supply closet the size of her high school dark room, the place where people went to smoke pot or give blow jobs. She could almost smell the vinegar burning her nostrils. She wore the lacy hot pants her coworkers had given her. Immediately, she realized there was a cheeky slit in the crotch, but she had no other alternative. She clenched her thighs shut. Her breasts, heavy and full, felt absurdly mammalian in her hands.

Mercifully, he got to work. For the photographer, there was no such thing as an extreme act of vanity. He led her into his studio, black drapery, umbrella light. He set up the shoot. As he spit out instructions, neck over shoulder, how to best position her feet to elongate her torso, how to maximize whatever angles were left, she felt disembodied. Her arm flattened her chest like a blackout strip. Was she subject or object? Is this what motherhood would be like? Separated from herself, her mind floated to the night that landed her here, she and her husband tumbling home, drunk, crashing into their practiced pattern, her unimaginative body assuming its position at the edge of the bed, until her ass dangled off, fighting gravity as he hooked her feet onto his hairy shoulders, like a gyno exam. Afterward, he collapsed atop her like he'd been shot.

The photographer zeroed in on her belly, tight and round. He told her to clutch the swell of her stomach like a golden egg. Norman knelt before her with a small bottle of baby oil, to shine her up for the light.

"Mother may I?" He asked, on his knees,

palms out to touch. She didn't laugh. She could feel the wind in the seat of her shorts. In what universe were crotchless underpants erotic? She did not want him rubbing anything on her. Movement rippled through her, a foot, a fist. She was no exotic fruit.

"I can't," she said, stepping back.

"That's cool," the photographer said, dusting off the dejection. As he stood, his knees creaked. He wiped his greasy hands on a hand towel. "It takes a certain kind of woman."

"This isn't me," she said.

"Don't apologize." He handed her a plush robe and flipped on the electric kettle in the alcove kitchenette. She sat on the couch as he prepared her cup of chamomile. She lifted his hefty portfolio into her lap. He really was good at what he did. While she flipped through the cellophane pages, he drafted up a store credit. Stood over her bowed head and handed her the slip. She demurred. “Take it,” he insisted. The paper flapped like a bird. They couldn’t look at each other. He told her, “There’s no expiration date.”

• • •

SHE RETURNED once the baby arrived. The baby looked like a wrinkled, humorless old man, and behaved accordingly. The baby complained all the time. She could practically hear her baby sending back the soup. She no longer slept. It was beyond her wildest imagination, weeks upon months of not sleeping, a military torture technique, a physical impossibility, and yet, all the same, it felt fitting, the not-sleeping, as if she’d entered a world where dreams came to die. The baby latched onto her breast like a permanent fixture. She was a milk machine. She was a repository of want. A reservoir of tears until she wasn't. Until, like all sources, she dried up. Work receded to a distant memory. The magazine shuttered. She was not going anywhere. She was going to her baby. Her husband had no patience for this nonsense. He had to get up in the morning and function like a real person. What else did she have to do? She was a mother. She heeded the cries. She sat in the rocker they'd custom-upholstered in anthropomorphic frogs and she held her baby, this child that she nourished and grew, her baby who somehow already knew life would disappoint you.

In these dark, muzzy hours, she googled Norman Wax. He had a fancy new website, multiple social media handles, and that's not all. Call it serendipity. Call it dumb luck. He'd caught a tech giant on a park bench contemplating his coffee as pigeons scrounged for crumbs by his feet. The image had gone viral. Billionaires: they're just like us! Everyone is oblivious to what's beneath them. The shot landed him the provocative final cover of a shuttering glossy—a drug-addled ingenue draped in the American flag—and now he was riding the wave. There he was on the arm of an actress, a model, an NYC it-girl. He was no longer just a photographer; he was a star-fucker. He must be fucking them all, fucking the assistants, how else did anyone get anywhere? She scrolled through image after image produced by someone else's camera: Norman Wax walking down the street, canoodling a neck, at a Yankees game, at an art opening, beanie-clad, clinking beers.

This clinched it. Norman Wax would take her baby's pics. On his website, he had a designated page full of babies. Babies dressed as chickens as avocados as sunflowers. Famous people's babies with names like Harlequin and Sage. Her photographer had influence. Her photographer levied opportunity. Her photographer resisted categorization. He was nimble. The man had range. Who could afford to be just one thing?

She wrestled her baby into a lion's mane. He took one look and refused.

"I'm not condoning this Hallmark crap," he said. "You're better than that."

"I'm not," she pleaded, her eyes red and bleary. She thought: *I'm no good.* The jagged birth scar along her lower abdomen itched. "Please," she said, looking at him. He evaded her gaze. She did not wish to argue or think. "It's a baby announcement. Do me a solid here."

"You're the client," he shrugged, and did what she said.

• • •

WHEN THE SECOND CHILD turned three, they scheduled a family portrait. It took months for him to fit her in. By now his studio had moved uptown to the parlor floor of an extra-wide brownstone on the east side where he also lived.

"Look at you," he said.

"Look yourself," she said. Heavy, gilded frames hung on the walls. The images: a mix of editorial, celebrations, limited-edition sneakers, and custom commissions.

"Aspirational," she said.

"Everyone wants a tailor-made version of their life," he said.

Like everyone, her family wore white. It made her think of that Bee Gees album. As if all they needed was angel wings.

The photographer tried his best. He arranged them affectionately. He cracked corny jokes to loosen them up, to elicit spontaneity, to capture the family in their natural state, but there was only so much he could do. Her oldest was shy. Her youngest was cranky. Of course, she was pregnant again. Her face shiny, her hair greasy. She would always be pregnant. Her husband kept taking calls outside.

Eventually, she followed her husband onto the stoop.

"Can't you be present, just once?"

"I am present," her husband said. "This is as present as it gets. Why is it so important? What are you trying to prove?"

"Where is your passion?!?"

It came out shrill. She could feel the photographer appear through the front bay window, hidden beneath his lens. She could have sworn she heard a click.

When they rejoined the shoot, she said, "I'm sorry. I'm a mess."

"You're beautiful," he said, stepping close. "You're my favorite subject to shoot."

She believed him. It never occurred to her that he might repeat this line to anyone else.

He tucked a hair behind her ear. She accepted a tissue.

"Where were we?" Her voice drifted off.

As might be expected, the photos were shit. The photographer had become a big shot, but he was no miracle worker. In the proofs her family looked like angry bots. But everything could be cropped and filtered at no extra cost. They found one that was good enough to slap on a holiday card—*from our family to yours*—where it would meet its fate beneath a fridge magnet, in the stack of junk mail, in the recycling bin.

• • •

YEARS PASSED. Milk teeth fell out, adult teeth muscled in, children stumbled through countless stepping-up ceremonies, singing about railroads or dreidels. Periodically, she'd come across his photo credit in the well-thumbed rags at the hair salon. The issues were outdated. As luck would have it, the media industry crumbled just as he was breaking in. No one was immune. Who could compete with stock imagery? Everyone was back where they started. Sure enough, when she wandered over to his website, she found herself frozen in time in his featured gallery, in the greenhouse from her sister's wedding, the bare shoulder from her own, a blurred outtake, like the arc of the moon captured from a great distance, unrecognizable to anyone else.

• • •

OCCASIONALLY, she'd see Norman Wax in real life. Second weddings, 40th birthday parties, anniversaries. It surprised her at first.

"Hey, big macher!" She raised her cocktail.

"Smoke and mirrors," he shrugged.

"Don't act coy," she said.

"What can I say, I'm a *simcha* animal."

"A beast!" she teased.

"A beast with a mortgage."

Smile.

Click.

"I have a wife now," he said.

She dropped her half-eaten pig-in-a-blanket onto a napkin. Covered her mouth as the steam escaped, dusted the greasy flakes off her fingers. "Get out! That's great."

"Yeah?"

"Yeah! I'm happy for you."

"Are *you*?"

• • •

ONCE SHE HIT THE bar mitzvah circuit, there was no avoiding each other. For a pair of years, they saw each other practically every month. There was comfort in consistency. He was always reliably there, in the entrance, capturing guest arrivals, leaning against an artificial column for the emcee announcement of the bar mitzvah boy, the party space decked out like a concert arena, buzzing with lights, glow sticks, adolescent heat.

"We can't keep running into each other like this," he'd say. And she'd smile. And maybe they'd stare at each other for a second longer, their gaze locking before he lowered his to his viewfinder for a pic and flit. This was the nature of the job. From the confetti poppers to the game room to the dramatic release of balloons, he flitted, snapping all the way, his a strange and frenetic mating dance, like a clown act paired with disappearance, with teleportation, he was nowhere and everywhere, which made her wait, she was always waiting, willing his return, watching him out of the narrow of her eye, acutely aware of her body in space, how she stood, hip out, clutching the long thin stem of one glass then another, stacking cubes of sushi, sliding off skewers of meat, clapping to the *hora*, shuffling through line dances, trussed in boas, in giveaway shades, until sure enough, he circled back.

"My muse!" he'd shout over the DJ, with a wink and a click. By the time her cheeks faded, Norman Wax would be off, performing his trick on someone else, everyone else, whatever it took to loosen up his subjects, to disarm them enough for a money shot.

"You again," she said, sidling up beside him when her oldest turned 13. She laughed at her own joke. After all, she'd hired him. There was something to be said for reliability. The photographer showed up. He wore his leather vest.

She leaned against his shoulder. It was warm and damp. She was a little drunk. Maybe a little more than a little.

"Look at you," he said, his voice low and slow. "Look who has it all."

"Look all you want," she said boldly, tittering on heels. "Look at us."

"My wife," he said. "She's having a baby. I'm going to be a dad."

And then, before she could blink: "Say 'cheese!'"

• • •

CUE THE SEASONS. Death, divorce, natural disaster—piercing and isolating quiet. Happy occasions ground to a halt. There was nothing to do but weather what came. The algorithms were winning. Last time his website popped up in her feed, all evidence of their photographic history had been shifted off his home page.

• • •

IT ALWAYS HAPPENS LIKE THIS: the minute you stop thinking about someone, there they are, pushing a child in a nubuck swing in the playground nestled in the heart of the park. For years, she'd run past the playground without pause, but a niggling injury had hampered her. A new coffee kiosk had sprung up where she'd once picnicked with the kids. There were countless options: hot lattes or cold brews, freeze-dried or oxygenated. The million dollar question: *what did she want?* It was a breezy summer day. Iced, the barista decided for her, handing her a cup with a napkin shrugged around it wet as a strip of papier-mâché. Sipping, she strolled over to the wrought iron fence that gated in families like animals at a zoo. Hey, she didn't say. Norman Wax! She didn't have to, for as he gazed out toward the swing, following the rise of his child pumping higher and higher into the sky, he caught sight of her standing there, staring. Plump little legs crashed back onto him. Whoosh! He caught and released. This was life's rhythm. His arm shot up in salute. *Look at you*, she mouthed. The photographer's eyes looked tired yet twinkly. He smiled, waved.

SLAUGHTERHOUSE RULES

THE EMPIRE KOSHER CHICKEN FACtory was a late addition to the Camp Masad intersession field trip. Typically, the pubescent group of *tzofim* ("scouts") attended a minor league ball game following the annual July pilgrimage to the Baseball Hall of Fame in Cooperstown, but this year the Red Barons happened to be the road, which meant there were a few extra hours to kill (hehe) before their expected arrival at Temple Beth Shalom in Harrisburg.

Back in Harrisburg, the Shabbaton would eventually unfold like all the others: withered chicken for dinner and circle dancing, sleeping bags unfurled like long tongues on the sanctuary floor. The late-night scramble for a hook up. A raid on the grape juice, a search for the hidden Manischewitz. Good clean fun. Haley hated it. She was not a camp person. Don't even get her started on God.

Her mother said it would be good for her (for whom? Haley or her mother?) to get out of the house that summer, after the *shiva*, to make friends, to meet a boy. Isaac was going. *You know, Isaac Abramovich from Hebrew School?* She knew. She went.

But first, the Chicken Factory. It was 1989. The imposing poultry plant was brand new after a suspicious fire had leveled the premises, and now tours were on offer, perhaps to help alleviate the costs of the rebuild. The bus pulled into the empty lot. Everyone grew antsy waiting while Rich, the division head, went inside to inquire whether a group of their size could be accommodated at the last minute. Moments later, he jogged back with a stack of glossy pamphlets and a bag of museum-style buttons. Campers shoved into the bus aisle to be tagged then they piled off.

"You'll stay with me," Haley's counselor Naomi said, with a meaningful shoulder squeeze. It was a statement not a question. Naomi was a vegetarian, Haley had a dead dad, so the two were one and the same. Skinny-mini-Vicki stayed put, too, with her wraparound hairy arms and her strict diet of milkshakes. No one wanted to risk further damage to her already fucked-up relationship to food. She sat across from Haley scowling into the yarmulke she was crocheting, the little blue disc the size of a foreskin and slowly widening in girth with each furious spin around her thumbs.

To cut costs, Camp Masad hired a low-rent school bus whose lack of shock absorption had made everyone queasy on the twisty back roads from the Poconos. The vehicle nearly got stuck in a ditch during an emergency roadside bladder evacuation not far from Three Mile Island before swinging into Arby's, where counselors looked the other way as campers loaded up on unkosher roast beef sandwiches as tall as the food chain logo's hat. The bus smelled of 40 thirteen-year-olds in a humid six-hour stew. Haley pinched down the windows and slumped in her seat. The vinyl was the color of the bottom of the ocean: oxygen-less blue.

Even the bus driver stood heavily, hiked up his pants, and left for a smoke. Naomi, Vicki, and Haley were the only ones left behind. Beside her, Naomi was embroidering a thick friendship bracelet against her clipboard, fingers deftly whipping through figure 4's. "I have extra string," she said, without breaking her rhythm. "Take as many colors as you want."

"I'm okay," Haley said, shaking her head.

It was well-intended, if warped logic: the assumption that because she'd lost her father (as if he'd simply wandered off) she'd entertained enough death for a while. She'd met her quota. As if by steering clear of the slaughterhouse, Haley might be spared additional grief; insulated from greater violence. It was too late for that, homies. Death was violent. Grief was her BFF. She could have protested, insisted, trailed after Isaac's falsetto, *"The Magical Murder Tour is hoping to take you away!"* but she didn't. Instead, Haley looked out the window. The enormous drab facility rose and rose.

• • •

INSIDE, THE GROUP WAS in for a treat. Their orthodox Willy Wonka wore a stained lab coat and a suede yarmulke. His reddish beard was neatly trimmed. He rubbed his palms and smacked his lips. "Who here has ever been to a slaughterhouse?" he asked with near delirious enthusiasm as the group dipped into a cardboard box of blue elastic booties, the kind distributed to prospective buyers at open houses, snapping them onto their sneakered and sandaled feet. With his hands behind his back, he rocked back and forth on his toes as they secured their smocks and hair nets. "You've never seen a place like this before." Already he was overpromising. Spewing history: the operation began in the Catskills, the locus of Jewish life, before moving to rural PA to fulfill its destiny of becoming the largest kosher facility in the country. The entirety of their fowl—that is, chickens *and* turkeys—were grown on the adjacent farm, making it a one-stop, all-inclusive resort: livestock, eggs, slaughterhouse, and packaging plant.

"Who knows what the word *kashrut* means?" he asked. Someone (Isaac, probably) whispered "salty dog shit" and the group erupted in laughter, so that Rich the division head had to raise his hand in remonstrance and annunciate, "Show a little *kavod*," before yielding the floor back to the tour guide who said, "*Kashrut* means ritual suitability."

He was just bubbling over with information, this dude. The *shochet*—our noble slaughterer—took great pride in his work, in his decisive single slice, in his nearly-bloodless style. Kosher slaughter was different from all other slaughters. Only the sharpest of knives was used on the animal's neck, guaranteeing an immediate loss of consciousness and death without suffering. "We specialize in the humane."

With that, the group pushed past the double doors into a shock of nipple-popping cold. Emma Clove was already complaining, "I can't bear it, I have Raynaud's!" eliciting tight, body-heat generating hugs from her obsequious bunkmates. Spanning the circumference of the killing room, the spectator floor was elevated, affording everyone a better view of the action below. The thick smell of metal hung in the air. Bird upon bird drifted by on dry cleaner hooks.

"After the slaughter, the inspection of organs and innards begins."

Campers walked by. Inspectors in hazmat suits with face shields and blue gloves labored at tables of taut, flayed carnage as if they were pouring over ancient Torah scrolls.

"Then they must remove all blood from the body. To accomplish this, the poultry is soaked in cold water—the purest of spring water!—for 30 minutes . . . but, you see, the cold temperature contracts the follicles, presenting a defeathering challenge. We've got our machines, of course, and we even have special employees whose sole purpose is to pluck stubborn, errant strands, and still, you've probably seen an odd hair or two at your *shabbos* table, amirite?"

• • •

HALEY FLIPPED THROUGH the pamphlet. Humane slaughter sounded like one of those paradoxical terms they'd learned in school (see also: jumbo shrimp) but there were many ways to die. Her father hadn't known what hit him. Everyone at shiva told her this, as if that were a comfort. It was easier to imagine bald birds on coat hangers than the truth of her father. She'd already spent the last two months picturing his body crushed between the pair of tractor trailers, like a trash compactor, on the Walt Whitman bridge. It was harder to picture the passenger beside him, a brunette in his office named Lonna, whose skull had been pulverized in his lap. Why were they headed to Gloucester City at 10 pm on a Tuesday? Were they checking out a new dental supplier? Restocking inventory from an existing vendor? Doing an emergency run on alloys and polishers? The office had said it was a business matter. No one was looking to make a horrible situation any worse.

She wondered what kind of shit Isaac was stirring up right now. With ghost-like skin and dark mossy curls, and with the beady eyes and affected drawl of Christian Slater, Isaac Abramovich was Camp Masad's uncontested rebel. There was something sadistic about him. Haley loved him. Right about now he was scooping up the fowl fluff and tossing it at Emma

Clove, who was squealing her rosaceous head off, provoking others into returning fire until they were all flinging feathers like loose down in a pillow fight.

• • •

HALEY'S BIG REBELLION: eating cheesesteaks with her dad in South Philly. They kept a kosher home, but there were loopholes, exceptions. Her dad said things like *Don't tell mom*, as they drove down to Jim's or Pat's for a fully loaded log of meat juiced up with peppers and onions. Her mother was always harping on him about his cholesterol, his LDLs. She'd started buying those fake eggs that came in a milk carton. For daddy's health, she'd say. We want him to stick around for a while.

The cheesesteaks were their secret ritual. It was, Haley assumed, their one cheat from a stringent life of rules and regulations. Her dad grumbled that all the righteous mumbo jumbo merely justified price gouging. *$20 a pound for brisket?* But her mother was a stickler. If she'd had her druthers, their kitchen would have sported two dishwashers and two sinks. Her dad called it extreme. And extremism, he said, was the root of all evil. Religion was the cause of all wars. So they made compromises. Dad could do whatever he wanted outside the home provided he didn't bring anything verboten under their roof. The greasy blend of meat and cheese always made Haley feel a little sick afterward, the flagrant commingling after a lifelong diet of separation. The law prohibited bathing the animal in the mother's milk or something, which sounded like some version of "don't shit where you eat." But it was totally worth it for the fleeting pleasure.

Apparently, the brunette, Lonna diPaulo, was the new tech in the office. Born and bred in South Philly, she was a single mother of three.

At her father's gravesite, while shoveling dirt into the pit, Haley overheard someone say that Lonna's mother, poor thing, would now have to spend her retirement years raising her angry, orphaned grandkids.

Involuntary manslaughter had been the ruling. They were killed by a drunk trucker who'd drifted at the wheel, accidently pushing them into another oversize tractor trailer hauling Chiquita bananas. Autopsies confirmed their deaths had occurred instantaneously upon impact. They didn't struggle and they weren't at fault, allowing the bereaved to focus on the transgressions of the living as opposed to the transgressions of the dead.

• • •

HAVOC WAS BUILDING in the butchering room. As the tour guide sputtered on about cuts and quarters, someone *(guess)* had picked up a chicken foot from the floor and shoved it down Phyllis Schwartz's back. Phyl The Pill did not take it lightly, immediately giving chase, bringing the whole raging mob with her down the narrow passageways. The metal grates clanged beneath their feet. Counselors urged them to slow down and to exercise caution as they slipped and slid on the sluice of blood and guts, but the tour guide clutched his belly, straining the buttons of his lab coat as he laughed. "You should have seen my last group of yeshiva boys." The ruckus did little to interfere with the productivity of the slaughterhouse. No one could hear them above the din of the machines, the whir of the fans, and the assembly line that sorted the parts—split breasts, quartered legs, whole hens. These cuts were then laid onto Styrofoam beds and vacuum wrapped, blessed once more for good measure, stamped with the rabbinical seal, and shipped off to a supermarket near you.

• • •

ONCE, WHEN SHE WAS LITTLE, Haley's dad took her to Hershey Park. The best part about being an only child was that she always had him all to herself. She never had to share. At Chocolate World, they took a motorized tour through the history and manufacturing process of the iconic candy bar. Her dad kept a stash of miniatures—Crackles, Mr. Goodbars—tucked in his bottom right desk drawer behind a clutter of dental impressions. Her mother never checked. Cocoa pumped through the vents as they inched through the simulation of plastic kisses, sheathed and unsheathed. The place smelled like a scented eraser. The tour was neither a thrill ride, nor a factory showcase, nor much of a light show. The whole experience was a letdown. "I know how you feel, Hal," her dad said, offering up a damp palm of free samples as a consolation. The chocolate tasted like chalk. "But someday you'll be tall enough to ride the Super-Duper Looper."

• • •

NAOMI HANDED HALEY a box of apple juice and a half-eaten sleeve of crackers. It reminded her of nursery school. Haley remembered tracing branches on brown construction paper, the blessings for the fruit of the trees. Camp Masad was big on blessings. There was a blessing for everything, from seeing a rainbow to taking a dump. Thank the lord for my unblocked orifices, as if the anus were a starburst portal to the sky. Rich said you did not need to believe in a higher power to express gratitude for all things everywhere. A blessing for snack time—a sort of catch-all through which her counselor Naomi's lips now moved. Amen. The graham crackers were stale as cardboard from last week's campfire.

Vicki hissed, "How can you eat at a time like this? Our group is—*literally*—a Nazi squad enacting an SS march through a concentration camp."

Years later, DreamWorks would make a fortune off an animated allegory of anthropomorphic chickens trying to escape from a barbed wire prison farm, and Haley would think of Vicki. Did she feel validated or exploited? Haley would wonder if skinny-mini-Vicki had stopped starving herself by then, if she'd converted to more mindful consumption, honoring the painstaking path of the food chain, plant and animal alike, from farm to table. If she still saw the imprint of genocide everywhere.

Right now, however, Haley was thinking about Isaac. He was already on probation, skating on thin ice. His outbursts and antics were ascribed to shoddy parenting—an absent father, a cancer-stricken mother, older brothers who bullied him ruthlessly until they left home. Causation offered containment. Answers to the unanswerable. As if everything could be explained by something else. Her father's death: an Act of God? Lonna: an act of protest against a rule-ridden home? Haley had no clue. All she knew was it felt reckless to outsource responsibility, to play the blame game, to displace desire like that.

She and Isaac weren't friends. They definitely weren't dating. They were at opposite ends of the social spectrum—he was visible and she was invisible. He wasn't exactly popular, or even well-liked, but people either went along with him—the mode of least resistance—or avoided him. Whereas Haley did not exist. But it was Isaac who, during last night's evening activity of "Jerusalem Bazaar," leaned into her and whispered "*Nakba*" hot into her ear. At first she thought this was something dirty, a come on, a proposition, something they might do together. Her eyes widened, the skin on her neck flushed with heat. "I bet you don't even know what it is," he dared her. She didn't answer. He shook his unruly curls. "The hypocrisy. Don't you see? All we ever get is one side of the story."

She sucks her juice box until it is concave. She measures time in the growth of Naomi's friendship bracelet, the pattern of V's stitched together to form diamonds. God's eyes. She watches Naomi's fingers whip through the pattern as if they were driven by some great purpose.

In September Haley would enter 8th grade. At least she'd had her bat mitzvah last fall, back when her family was still intact. Her bat mitzvah had been during Sukkot, the harvest holiday devoted to cycles and change. The congregation gathered under the temple's pergola for blessings and bread. Bees backstroked in the wine. Her mother wore a wool dress on an unseasonably warm day, sweat beading on her lip as she held Haley's father's hand. He looked strangled in his tie. Together they toasted their newly-adult daughter with that song by The Byrds: *to everything, turn, turn, turn.*

Isaac had made a scene at her party, pouring all the abandoned cocktails into one glass in a monster suicide then chugging it. When he lit up a cigarette in the coat closet, it had been her father who, to Haley's mortification, gently escorted him out, draping Isaac's rumpled blazer over his narrow shoulders and calling him, "My son."

• • •

EVENTUALLY, the tour came to an end, bottoming out into the gift shop—stuffed chickens, cookbooks, chef's hats—that led to the exit. The scouts busted free, some sprinting toward the bus, others zigzagging in a sort of drunken daze, their arms slung over each other, newly bonded after having lived through "the journey" together. The tour guide bid them farewell at the doorway, waving fervently, "Come back soon!"

The bus door sighed open. As the group clambered on, they looked changed, feral, like they'd survived the wilderness, or as if they were somehow complicit, as if they'd carried out the ritual slaughter themselves. "Ah-mazing!" They were saying. And: "I'm never eating again!" Becca Clove paused at Haley's seat and spoke to her for the first time that whole month: "You're lucky you missed it."

That night in Harrisburg, and for the rest of the summer, the slaughterhouse escapade would reverberate. Who would become a vegan, a yogi, a sustainable farmer? Who would become a lawyer and who would become a shrink? Would there be a *shochet* among them? A rabbi? A senator? A globalist tech bro? Who would find faith, who would abandon it, who would intermarry, who would join the army, who would join a kibbutz, who would join a masthead, who would join a dental practice, who would condemn the diasporic ideology in which they'd been raised?

Isaac was the last to board. The bus couldn't move until everyone had taken their seats. Isaac Abramovich was taking his sweet defiant time, juggling in the aisle. "Sit down, psycho!" Phyl the Pill shouted, but he just went on tossing yellow things in the air like the Swedish chef as if he didn't hear her.

Chicken's feet. Rubbery, clawed, joint ends bare and round as a translucent moon. Haley had read in *Weird Science Facts!* (left in the communal bunk stall) that fingers were once part of a whole webbed palm. Individuation, that is, splitting into digits, occurred when the cells that once joined them started dying. If it weren't for the death of all that connective tissue, we'd all be walking around with mittened hands, humans and chickens alike. On the flip side, she read, cancer was an excess of life, an overgrowth of multiplying cells. Isaac's mom had breast cancer, but Haley wasn't about to tell him that too much life in a body could kill you.

Rich corralled Isaac and the bus hit the road. They would be in Harrisburg before sundown. Haley's stomach growled. She could almost taste the roast chicken sitting in its oily orange glaze, the platters of wet kasha and bowties that awaited them. As the bus peeled out onto the gravel, Rich recited *tefilat ha derech*, tripping over the foreign words, undeterred, issuing a blessing for a safe journey. She'd never know where her father had been headed on that bridge.

"Hey, Haley," Isaac said, popping up in his seat. Arm cocked, eyes blazing. For a split second the entire bus went silent. "Catch!" The foot flumped onto her lap. Detached from its source, it looked like a toy, like one of those gag key chains whose plasticine digits could be bent into a gesture of obscenity. How easy it was to forget it was once part of a living, breathing thing.

HIDDEN SAINTS

WHO WOULD BELIEVE IT? YOUNG Shimi Shem Tov had been selected—hand-picked by the acting chief rabbi!—to open a Chabad-Lubavitch outpost on the Greek island of Zakynthos so that any Jew—any wanderer in need of a warm meal or clean bed, a home away from home—could stay by him and rest.

This was a great honor, an honor befitting a greater man. When the rabbi—not *The Rebbe*, Menachem Mendel Schneerson, may his memory be a blessing—but The Rebbe's right-hand man and chief secretary, called him into his office at 770 headquarters, Shimi assumed he'd been caught dozing during Musaf again. Dust particles alighted in the afternoon sun from the enormous bay window, casting Rabbi Krinsky in obscure shadow. Shimi blinked and blinked, and still, darkness. His gaze shifted dreamily toward the mystical haze winking above Krinsky's head. While studying, Shimi's mind often wandered to the vastness of the universe, how we are all but a scattered speck of dust floating on an infinitely spinning planet.

Rabbi Krinsky did not smile. He leaned forward, resting his substantial beard on his tented, liver-spotted hands. He called Shimi, "my son." It was true that The Rebbe, having no children, had left no successor. It was also true that, even as they mourned the immense chasm in the universe created by the immeasurable loss of their spiritual leader—a void that could not be filled by mere mortal shoes—the Lubavitcher Rebbe's lifelong mission would not be in vain. As they fervently prayed for the world to come, Krinsky would ensure that Schneerson's vision of *dira betachtonim*, of godliness in the material realm, would not only persist but expand, *b'zrat hashem*.

The year was 1998. Shimi could still feel the great rupture of The Rebbe's death four years prior. How his Lubavitch community had wailed and wept, filling the double-wide streets of Eastern Parkway as if on Simchat Torah, only there was no *simcha*, no dancing, no singing, only a river of tears. Had The Rebbe truly been the Moshiach, as many claimed? Shimi joined in the chorus but held no convictions. All he knew was that The Rebbe had been a mighty man, a performer of miracles, from conjugal matches to fertility and everything in between. His parents credited The Rebbe with plucking them from the lawless streets of Berkeley, California. How desperately lost they'd been until they were found.

Like everyone else, Shimi had davened, beat

his breast, surrendering to the wellspring of grief. Through prayer, he experienced humility and expansiveness at once, the lonely bowel sounds of his body and the chorus of the collective. He felt the most himself and yet utterly irrelevant, as if he might slip between the gathered waves of energy and disappear. With the rest of his classmates, he'd spilled out onto the streets to paper the neighborhood, in blessed memory, so that The Rebbe's eternal face hugged every lamppost and crosswalk box, every storefront and grate, every inch of exposed wall in honored perpetuity.

At 20, Shimi's sparse, wiry beard barely sprouted over his chin. Fresh out of yeshiva, his face, greased with Potato Stix, hosted a colony of pimples.

"It is your time," Krinsky said gravely. Shimi crossed his right leg over his bony left knee, his right arm over his left, to evoke rabbinic contemplation. He scratched his elbow. None of it made sense. For one, he'd been the youngest in his class. His mother, pregnant with the twins, had been eager to get him out from underfoot and into some structured schooling. He was hardly an exceptional student. Too literal, or not literal enough, depending on the teacher. Mediocre at best, he did not burn the midnight oil with feverish curiosity or take any real initiative, content to coast on the coattails of some of his more ambitious classmates, looking out the window, listening to the rhythmic drop of a pinky ball against a hard brick wall, imagining himself on the outside instead of stuck in. Like this, he became a rabbi.

And now someone saw great promise in him. He had been tapped! Shimi stroked his underwhelming beard. This was a mystery, but life was mysterious.

His *yidishe neshama*, Krinsky said, would serve

him well as an emissary of God. Gentiles had their Peace Corps, their AmeriCorps. Mormons their missions. Lubavitcher outreach was driven not by conversion, but by the urgent, unrelenting desire to amend the loss of six million by drawing in the drifted, like his own formerly hippie parents (who'd taken the last name Shem Tov after the great 18th century mystic), bringing them all back into the fold.

The men shook hands. Promises were made. Headquarters would furnish him with everything: housing, plane tickets, a livable stipend, a long-distance calling card, a framed photo of the Rebbe himself, a wife, a map.

• • •

SHIMI SAT BEFORE HIS new bride-to-be. She'd come from Jerusalem, the only daughter in a family of brothers, from a long line of rabbis.

Pious, modest, quiet—or shy—Shimi couldn't discern the difference. They spoke Yiddish. It was not much of a conversation. Her name was Esti. At the corner café on Kingston Avenue, he ordered a thick slice of marble cake—still moist! —with two forks. Two cans of Coke. He pushed the paper off a straw and casually handed it to her. She shook her head, demurely peeled her own.

There was a wedding, a send-off, a series of rituals, community-wide gatherings, an awkward consummation, fumbling in the dark that left Shimi feeling more empty than full. He had so much to learn! The newlyweds stayed at Krinsky's in separate beds, Esti in the kitchen with the rebbetzin mostly, her scalp itching slightly beneath the weight of her exorbitant new wig. Throughout the waiting period, Esti never unpacked. Her suitcase sat stoutly in the foyer.

Two months later, they were gone.

Greece, they were headed for Greece! Not just any Greece. Already Chabad had an established presence in Athens, plus a sweet set-up on Crete, which attracted tourists from Australia to Los Angeles, as well as typical, peripatetic post-army types from Tel Aviv.

No, they were headed not to the Mediterranean or the Aegean but to the Ionian Sea. To the island of Zakynthos. Krinsky explained that this was one of the Rebbe's dying wishes. The island, shaped like an arrowhead, held particular significance. Did Shimi know why? Shimi curled his sidelock. *Zakynthos?* He could barely find the Bronx on a map.

Krinsky licked his pale lips. The story of Zakynthos has much to teach us, Krinsky whispered. Shimi had to lean over Krinsky's enormous desk to hear him, catching a whiff of smoked fish.

This is what he told him:

During the Holocaust, the entire Jewish population of this 40-mile island was spared. All around them, on islands near and far, as well as on the mainland, some 40,000 were rounded up and deported, 87 percent to Auschwitz alone, never to return. The entire Juderia of Rhodes was eradicated, did Shimi know that? Shimi did not. Not so on Zakynthos. The island's mayor and metropolitan bishop forged a secret pact. They became, how do you say, conscientious objectors. They would not heed orders. Imagine the camaraderie. They would rather die than comply. When the Nazis demanded that they turn over a list of Jews, they refused, submitting instead a list that included only their own two names, with the note, "Here are the Jews you requested," while tucking away the entire population in rural mountain villages. It was like this that humanity prevailed. All 275 were saved.

Did Shimi understand the value? Quickly,

he applied *gematria* to the number 275 as if to unlock its spiritual secret: *bet, zion, heh. Theft? Plunder?* He shook his head.

"What became of them after the war?" Shimi asked. Reports indicated that most Jews left for Athens, left for Palestine. And yet. How many of the hidden still inhabited the island while living secular, assimilated lives? This, Shimi would have to determine. Thus, his mission was mapped. He would welcome the weary to share in the mitzvah of Shabbos, of course, but mostly, he was to become a kind of detective. A Poirot—Shimi looked blank—A Sherlock Holmes? An Inspector Gadget! —seeking the descendants of those who'd survived. There was no further discussion.

They left in March. On the flight to Athens, Esti looked out the window while quietly weeping. Shimi, too, felt a giant swell of emotion, 40,000 feet high, above the cloud line. He draped their heavy wool coats over their laps. He did not ask her if this was what she wanted. Want, her desires, how she envisioned her own life—these were not questions to be entertained. Everything they did was in service to Hashem. Just think, he recalls saying, you'll be closer to your family in Jerusalem. A short plane ride, a long ferry. He meant this as consolation. You can visit! They can visit! We will break bread together.

From Athens they boarded a bus to the port town of Kyllini. An hour and a half ferry brought them to Zakynthos—Zante, for short. The ferry was a far cry from the water taxis circling Ellis Island. Shimi had never been on a boat of this size. A boat that carried four-door sedans, delivery trucks, mopeds! Waves lapped the portholes. The sea churned, heaving them up and down, like the Pirate Ship amusement ride amid all the *goyishe naches* at Coney Island. Shimi felt his stomach seize. His mouth filled with the taste of the tuna sandwich he'd polished off earlier on the plane. Had he squeezed his bride's hand? Had he exclaimed, What an adventure! He cannot remember. They spoke in Yiddish, but they would need to rely on English if they were to make it on Zakynthos. Before he left, his father had given him a pocket Greek dictionary the size of Tehillim, which he'd slipped inside his inner suit pocket. All around him families were eating, drinking, smoking. Laughter erupted from a meaty pack of Brits in matching striped rugbys. Air, Shimi indicated, thumbing toward the exit, leaving Esti alone in her plastic bucket seat while he joined the other travelers above deck.

It was then that he felt it, while gazing at the enormity and anonymity of the vast blue sea. *Time is the distance between two places,* he thought as he stared into the great distance before them. He couldn't remember where he'd heard that.

Maybe from his mother? He closed his eyes and welcomed the cool March sun. Greek mythology wasn't something taught in yeshiva. There was no place for stories of pagan worship. *Hercules*, he'd seen the animated film, but he couldn't remember if Hercules was human or a God. Was he the one who held up the world? Shimi closed his eyes, picturing the cartoon that his siblings watched. Golden flesh, loin cloths, bulging muscles, defined abs. An immodest display, but it kept them quiet for two hours. When he opened his eyes, a bird swooped in and perched on the ferry's railing. A dove, Shimi decided. A good omen, a blessing for safe passage. He didn't get close enough to see if it was just an ordinary gull.

At the port, a mob of taxicabs was muscling for position. By the time he retrieved their bags from the crowded luggage racks and dragged them to the curb, Shimi was in a sweat. He unfolded the damp piece of paper in his pocket with the smudged address of their future, the writing as small and as precise as a child's.

It was a treacherous drive. The taxi wound up and around the side of a mountain on a road unfit for two-way traffic, narrowly close to the edge. There was no guard rail. In the book of Bereshit, this rocky region was listed as Yavan, settled by descendants of Noah's son Japheth, but the table of nations was about as far as Shimi got in world geography. Stubborn clusters of olive trees clung to the hill, their spindly branches stretching toward the cliffs, but otherwise, there was limited vegetation, perhaps on account of the island's front-facing position toward the wind and the heat. Here and there was a goat, a patch of grass, a resilient desert flower. Esti clutched the grab handle. Shimi caught the driver eyeing them through the rear-view mirror as they climbed, the hairpin turns knocking around the luggage in the back, until they reached the top and the road leveled off onto unpaved dirt.

Suddenly, Esti shivered. She clutched Shimi's arm, flooding him with desire. "What is it, my wife?"

That's when he saw the first goat head, pierced on a barbed wire fence. Horned, intact, its long face narrow and furry. *Oy gut!* As they rumbled down the road, the heads multiplied: some fresh, some rotting, some half decomposed with their eyes plucked out, flies buzzing, caving in like forgotten fruit. Heads were strung along the fence like Christmas lights. Shimi leaned forward to ask the driver: what does it all mean? The driver did not answer. Shimi raised his voice and asked again. Still, crickets. Maybe the driver did not understand. Shimi pointed. Why the goat heads? Goat! The driver nodded. Goat! Many, many goat. With that, he made a sharp turn down a dusty embankment and stopped in front of a white plaster church topped with a royal blue dome.

Home, sweet home.

Shimi paid the driver in drachmas and removed their suitcases from the trunk. They were to set up shop here, per Krinsky's orders, in this distant place on a craggy hill overlooking the turquoise sea, a place known for its endangered population of loggerhead turtles.

So what if Krinsky had left out a few details? What did it matter? God would provide. Nervously, Esti pointed to the cross on the roof. Shimi tried to placate her. It's okay, my bride, everything is how it should be. They were renting property from Dmitri Drakos, the region's reclusive goat herder. This abandoned house of worship sat at the edge of his ancestral land. The church was theirs. The goats, none of their business. Mostly, the herd stuck to their side of the road. They dotted the rugged hills. Shimi could hear them bleating. He could hear their bells jangling from their necks as the collies shepherded them along to more fertile pastures, although the notion of "fertile" was relative here on this harsh, dry land. One or two goats wandered into the barren yard, where Dmitri's mother now stood, dressed head to toe in widow black, leaning on her broom. Their very own caretaker! Wasn't it amazing, Esti? A cool breeze blew through their heavy clothes. They were not in Brooklyn anymore.

• • •

THE YOUNG COUPLE TOOK their time settling in. The whole world—their whole lives!—were ahead of them. Shimi embraced the pioneer spirit. We will build it! They will come! He would be like Noah, son of Lamech himself!

Every morning, he woke in his modest room and recited *modeh ani,* feet on the ground and gratitude in his heart. After he performed his daily ablutions and wrapped *tefillin*, binding the leather strap tightly to his forearm then weaving the letters *Shin Dalet Yud* through his fingers with its tail end (another word for God: *Nurturer*, aka *The Breasted One*), he sat with Esti on the cracked stone patio. Turkish coffee burbled on the stove top. Sometimes, they had fruit, a bit of bread. A kiss on the lips or cheek. No one was around. Then they parted. There was so much to do!

Quickly, Shimi learned his way around a hammer and nails. First, he hung the poster of the Rebbe. He put up *mezuzot*. Then he directed his attention to repairs. Painting, spackling, patching bits of peeling plaster. He purchased caulk to seal the leaking tub. He welcomed the physical toil, the chance to roll up his sleeves and direct his attention to cracks and tears, to do the necessary work. This was living, breathing Torah. Like the world's first couple, Adam and Eve, their labor was pure. Sometimes his eyes got wet for no reason, like when Esti cubed up cucumbers the size of baby teeth or baked golden loaves fluffy as pillows in the sun, their yeasty aroma putting him in the mood for love. He could picture them, husband and wife, anchoring the ends of a long sabbath table, and it felt right. They were *shluchim!* His purpose: loud and clear.

But other times, it all felt more muddled. Here he was, dropped on a Mediterranean island, sentenced to an alternate existence like a staged contestant on a reality show. On these days he could float up from his body and watch it perform the motions. The artifice ate at him. Perhaps everyone was a pawn at the mercy of some Supreme Player. He tried not to think. If he was being tested, then what was the test?

Meantime, with the mother of Dmitri the goat herder by her side, Esti turned the modest refectory into her kosher kitchen. The widow's name was Elena. Although she spoke almost no English, it was amazing how much common ground could be secured, how well a person could communicate by gesture alone. Together they industriously scrubbed the cabinets and countertops and glassware. They placed stones into pots, pots into the oven, and buried cutlery into the ground until it was acceptable for use.

Dmitri the fearsome goat herder, however, kept his distance. Elena indicated his house, set back far from the road, but Shimi wasn't sure where it was exactly. It was not visible from his residence, and he did not dare venture closer. He did not want to upset the man. Other than the putrid goat heads, the sound of *leria* bells, and the sporadic goat sighting, there was no sign of their proprietor.

Before long, their first Pesach was upon them. It was customary to invite in strangers for the Seder—Jew and non-Jew alike. When Shimi mentioned this to Elena, she fiercely shook her head, launching into rapid fire Greek that Shimi could not begin to parse. She shaped her arthritic hands into a heart then crunched her fist. From this, he inferred that Dmitri's heart had been broken, leaving him hardened like the cloistered beast of fairy tales who lived in his castle among talking clocks, another cartoon his siblings watched when his mother needed to lie down. The man must be lonely, Shimi thought. Goats did not fill the bed.

"Would you put in a good word?" Shimi persisted, mopping his brow. It would be an honor to host him. Elena studied his wide-eyed hope. Shimi knew this look. It was a look of pity, a look that said you don't know the first thing about this world.

The couple proceeded to prepare for the holiday. Some products would be flown in. The Chabad of Athens sent a shipment, which Shimi signed for at the port. Esti, with Elena's help, navigated the shopping, freeing him to focus on the stated goal of his mission: to gather guests from all over the island to their ceremonial table.

He went to the main square. A memorial to the metropolitan and the mayor had been erected here after the war, but the statues, along with the island's only synagogue, had been wiped out in the earthquake of 1953. What remained was a simple dedication to the righteous saviors: two stone pillars side by side. Shimi sat on a bench. Birds gathered at his feet. He reached into his pocket, and tossed out a handful of sunflower seeds, the shells long and pointy as beaks. It was a nasty habit, this snack, the sucking, the collection of wet shells, like chewing fingernails on the NYC subway, but it beat other habits, like overeating, like smoking. With seeds in his pockets, he would never go hungry.

It was a windy day in late April. An elderly man in an undershirt sat on a bench across from him holding a cane. A young woman with jet black hair leaned against the fence. Her kids chased each other in circles until they grew dizzy and collapsed onto each other like a heap of sticks.

In Brooklyn, jovial yeshiva *bochers* skipped door to door looking for signposts, slipping pamphlets in mail slots. They stood by the subway station saying, "Excuse me, are you a Jew?" On Pesach, they loitered outside grocery stores peddling handmade *shmura matzo*, going so far as to offer free boxes of the costly artisanal *matzo* in exchange for listening to their spiel. People were more likely to give of themselves if they'd already received something. But people were hard to come by on this quiet island. They barely looked at him. His pocket dictionary was useless. He couldn't read Greek. The phonetic translation was equally puzzling. *Evraikos? Evraikos? Evraikos? Evraikos?*

His squawks went unanswered.

Headquarters stepped in. Young, shaven men arrived with matching duct-taped suitcases and protective hat boxes. Their smell spilled out of their pores: salt, oil, adolescent sweat. It would be a holiday after all.

On the first seder night, after the plagues, after the pinky dips in wine, after the recitations of the four sons, after the feverish rendition of Dayenu, after the soup and gefilte fish, after the whole grand meal which Esti prepared with the help of Elena, the blessed woman, a presence arrived at the door just as they were rising from their chairs to welcome the prophet Elijah.

Chubby Yaakov Bronstein, with one hand on the doorknob, jumped back in surprise. *Eliyahu Hanavi!* The prophet himself!

Dmitri Drakos looked like a boxer. He was square and stocky, and his head was flattened at the crown, as if smashed by a heavy, fallen object. His face was wide, his nose ruddy. His arms bulged from his sides like pumped up balloons.

"Shimi?" he asked, his voice gruff and gravelly, an engine sputtering to a start.

Shimi jumped to his feet in delight. "Come in! You're just in time! Ela! Ela! Ela!" Of the little Greek he knew he thought it would be most effective if he repeated it.

"I am disturbing?" Dmitri asked in low, halting English.

"No disturbance. Not at all!"

Dmitri hesitated. Then he held up a bottle of clear liquid.

"Ouzo?"

"L'chaim!"

That night, they drank. On top of the mandated four cups of wine, they polished off the bottle of local liquor. They reclined on pillows against their folding chairs, their shoulders loosely sloping toward one another. Dmitri was older, perhaps 40. Double Shimi's age. Or maybe not. Islands age people. Circumstances age people. Shimi did not dare ask for his story. Why jeopardize a tenuous peace? Instead, they sat around the table refilling their shot glasses as Elena and Esti cleared the dishes around them, making trips to and from the refectory. The young men—boys, really—eventually rose to help. They had mothers, too. They stacked plates and wrapped platters with foil and placed them in the fridge. Almost all of them belonged to families where the daughters exclusively bore this labor, so they also soon abdicated these domestic tasks for the chapel and then later, in the pink of dawn, for the clear, bright sea.

Of course, the thought occurred to him. Could Dmitri Drakos be one of the lost Zakynthos Jews? Popping in like this felt more than serendipitous. It felt destined, *beshert*. But Shimi did not wish to offend his neighbor with direct interrogation. This line of questioning and other global concerns suddenly felt out of place on their quiet lump of rock where time stood still. Instead, they drank ouzo and smoked. They milked goats. They made cheese.

• • •

AFTER THAT FIRST PESACH, a great friendship formed. Dmitri's reserve opened Shimi's floodgates. He confessed hopes, dreams, frustrations, failures. Sometimes they rode into town in Dmitri's faded lime Datsun, their arms braced against open windows as the dust flew into their eyes. Nights, they clung to the bluff, listening to the gentle roll of the sea. His mission was proving harder than he'd thought. Where had all the descendants gone? To intermarriage, to assimilation, to another country or another island? It was as if they'd never existed. "You cannot bring back those who do not wish to be brought in," Dmitri said.

Shimi glanced at his friend in profile. He admired the offhanded stubble across his hardened jaw, the cross-pendant winking from a chain by his collar. Dmitri Drakos had no children, as far as he knew. There had been a woman, once. Elena had been a widow as long as Dmitri could remember. His father and siblings were rarely mentioned. Eventually, after two dozen shots of anise, Shimi broached the matter of the goat heads, betraying his constellation of fears: idolatry, heresy, Satanic ritual.

Dmitri smiled his rare smile. "I see this on Creta one time. I do not kill for the head. No part is wasted. The goats have already dead."

The goats were meant as a deterrent, that's all.

To signal *private property.* To ward off unwanted visitors, bandits who wanted to skim the herd. It was ironic how at odds the men's agendas were, with Dmitri determined to *keep out* and Shimi called upon to *bring in.*

• • •

AS IT TURNED OUT, Zakynthos was less remote than Shimi had thought. Tourists arrived in early May, whipping the region into a hormonal froth. Because of its proximity to the mainland, Zante attracted local Greeks as well as heaps of foreign visitors, particularly from the UK, the Netherlands, and Germany. Clubs and bars cropped up all around Lagunas with names like Logger Heads or Smuggler's Cove or Shipwreck Beach.

During the high season, techno beats from the beachfront discos coursed through him, rising with the island wind, vibrating through their modest home. When he closed his eyes, Shimi pictured limbs of skin, bodies soldered together like liquid metal. Nobody ever had a face. It was pure fantasy.

In reality: he studied, he prayed. Clumsily, he made babies. If procreation was mandated, pleasure was elusive, catching him in spastic, near apologetic release. Esti never made a sound. Esti's body remained another unfamiliar land for which he had no map, which he was reluctant to explore, and which seemed, if not inhospitable, at least indifferent to his presence.

He was ruled by routine. Three prayer services a day, with meals built around them, except when the summer heat stole his appetite, leaving room for little more than a plum, a nose of bread. Elena assisted Esti in the kitchen until dusk, when she'd hang her cloth apron on a hook by the door, doling out a quiet nod with her nightly departure. The widow was not a hugger, which was a good thing, because there were laws against hugging. Laws against touch. Laws made the infinite finite. The circumscription of laws was a comfort. Laws removed all thought. Laws provided a framework, a security blanket. An insurance policy. A strait jacket. A noose.

A rusted moped sat parked on their property. How tricky could it be? Key in the top box; a pair of goggles slung over the handlebars. A twist in the ignition sputtered the machine to life. Shimi jerked it along the unpaved road until he got the hang of riding it, until he could make those hairpin turns without toppling over.

He drove to buy groceries: cucumber, tomato, onion. Feta. Items that could be ingested without a *hechsher* if one found oneself flung far from home. Shimi was a good Jew, but there was an exception for everything. Of course, they'd also schlepped over plenty of their own goods. A trunk of liverwurst. A valise of cured meats.

Friendly engagement was endemic to the Chabad spirit. He could not sit around waiting atop his little hill. Going into town was like entering the gates of Gehenna, but it was his job. Shimi Shem Tov, armored in Talmud, could resist the town's temptations. He looked but he did not touch. Tourist season had its benefits: budget-conscious travelers rarely refused a free meal or the promise of wine. But afterward, he'd feel hollow, as if he'd met cheap satisfaction in the arms of an indifferent prostitute. The indifference is what eroded him. Maybe Shimi was not charismatic enough. Maybe it was naïve to think he could spit into his little flute of faith and draw stray Jews out of the woodwork. What was he offering, exactly, other than a history of annihilation, a lifestyle of restriction, an indeterminate future peppered with hate? Where was the sell in that?

In those early months, emissaries from nearby

Croatia and Malta popped in to check on him. He was grateful for any company. Company was cause for celebration! Dmitri offered to get whatever Shimi needed. Lamb, Shimi requested, not realizing Dmitri would deliver a live animal. The slaughter was violent and quick and more emotionally charged than anything he'd ever done. One slice to the jugular, a fountain of blood. Merciful God. Shimi was now a *shochet.*

Shimi returned in the evening with the gruesome reek on him. He hosed himself off then drew a bath and still he could not remove the ripe smell from his fingernails. When he crouched over her, Esti turned her nose. Exhilarated, he wanted to tell her all about it, the fragility of life, the proximity of death, the awe of sacrifice, as if he were a high priest in the time of the Temple.

"I don't want to hear it," Esti said, clutching her belly. Her body inched toward the wall.

In this way, they became a family. The first baby was a boy, *baruch hashem*. There would be no *minyan*, but on the eighth day a *mohel* arrived from Athens with a stiff, black medical bag. Dmitri presented the child on a little pillow, and after the ritual circumcision, Shimi lowered his mouth to his son named Daniel and sucked the blood from the covenant wound while the *mohel* pocketed his son's foreskin to bury in a customary pot of Jerusalem soil.

Oh, how he loved being a father! He cradled baby Daniel in his arms, squeezed his thighs, his *pulkies* juicy and thick as drumsticks. He pumped him up and down overhead as if he were a *sefer* Torah. He couldn't get enough of the milky, sour smell, the grip of the little fist on his thumb. He felt that his heart might burst from his chest, shatter like a clay vessel into a million pieces. This was radical amazement: how his bedtime blunders had resulted in the miracle of life.

This made all that evening awkwardness worth it! Both he and Esti breathed easier when she shifted to the adjacent cot during her monthly bleed, grateful for the reprieve from expectation. Until the conjugal commandment resumed. And she was pregnant again.

Now, he and Esti had something to talk about. They talked about the baby. When the baby needed to eat or sleep or bathe. They talked about the color of his stool. They made grocery lists for the baby. They were always running out of something, in need of something else. Shimi fished in his pockets for the newly minted euro. Having a family would bring them closer, he assumed. This was the ingredient that had been missing.

They were fruitful. They multiplied. Twins ran in his blood. There was baby after baby, boy upon boy upon boy. The happy couple didn't keep track. It was superstitious to count one's blessings. There were babies in the crook of every arm. Esti cast a zombie stare into the fridge like she'd forgotten why she'd opened it. Elena bustled around them in black, stirring simmering pots, wiping smears of mashed peas off the floor.

Babies barely outgrew outfits before they fit the next baby. They passed down clothes, passed down pacifiers, passed down loveys. Shimi relished the human music. He dipped his spoon into porridge, into sweet potatoes. He made airplane noises. He rode the babies on his back bucking like a bronco. He davened with them, shrouding them beneath his prayer shawl, where they twisted the fringes, sucking on the ends. When Esti took to her bed, he puttered around the kitchen. He made eggs.

When the weather turned and the population nose dived, Esti and the children went to her parents in Jerusalem. On this they agreed. He would visit, of course.

But the land of milk and honey did not seem nearly as sweet as Zante. In the old city, people pushed and shook their fists. Even when they weren't angry, they shouted angrily, flicking wrists in a gesture both commonplace and seemingly profane. Shimi found himself irritable, anxious to return to his small outpost on a hill. Esti's extended family lived in a five-story building of Jerusalem stone, a place as stoic and cold as a mausoleum. They looked the same, they dressed the same, they hosted the same stern expressions and hardened opinions. Shimi felt suddenly out-of-place among all this likeness.

His brother-in-law grilled him.

How would they raise the boys? Shimi insisted that the children had each other. They were all so close in age. They stacked blocks, they crashed toy trucks, they crayoned the walls. On Fridays, they thumped out challah dough on stepstools beside Esti and Elena, their hair long and wild. Shimi was already mourning their first haircuts at the age of three. And then what? Did Shimi really think he could run a *cheder* in Zakynthos? Had the Mediterranean sun melted his brain?

The boys needed more. Back on the island, Shimi leased a car to get them out of the house and to give Esti a break. But with so many boys, and with only his two eyes, he was outnumbered. Inevitably, there were playground fights, careless falls, broken bones. Instead of alleviating her burden, he only compounded it.

The following summer, he gazed upon Esti with great sadness. She was not frolicking in the square. She was not packing a seaside picnic. She stayed inside perspiring miserably into her pantyhose. *If you love someone, set them free*, Dmitri said. Shimi was not sure he'd call this feeling love.

Esti couldn't look at him.

Go, he said. Go for you.

With that, she threw her arms around his neck. He felt an unprecedented surge of affection. Her breath in his ear. Thank you. She packed up the kids and left.

• • •

TO COMBAT THE ACHE of absence, he frequented town. He took out ads in the paper. He stared into the summery eyes of strangers. His baby brother Pinky had one of those picture books—*Where's Waldo?*—a dizzying maze of faces camouflaging a lone red and white hat in the crowd. Pinky used to leave it splayed beside the toilet, where it collected endless overdue library fees.

Stray cats brushed against his leg, their soft, tantalizing tails sending tingles up his spine. He was so rarely touched. He closed his eyes, spilling the bag of sunflower seeds from his lap. When he opened them again, a widow with trunk-like ankles was wagging her finger at him. *Huh?* He said, groggily, before realizing he'd made a mess of things. He mumbled an apology and fell to his knees, gathering up his chaos of seeds.

Back at the house, he got busy. He tidied the chapel, which was overrun with plastic toys. He repaired the roof. He tried to study, but he couldn't focus. Words made him sleepy. He opened book after book and dozed and dozed. He missed the healthy banter, the boyish antics, the passionate debates of his peers. How could he learn anything in a vacuum? Humans were social animals. He needed to socialize. He needed other people.

Dmitri could be erratic, unpredictable. Shimi learned to gauge his moods by the goat heads. A fresh head was a good sign. A sign of welcome. But when the heads were leaking and pitted with flies, Dmitri would not receive him. If they passed each other on the road, Dmitiri would eye him warily, like an intruder, as if they'd never met. Sometimes, Dmitiri would mumble to himself. When words were indecipherable, the message was clear: stay away. Shimi left a bottle of ouzo by the fence post and waited.

Like this, time expanded and collapsed. Time skipped the light fandango. Esti gave birth to another child, blessed be he. Shimi's beard grew. Summer stretched into fall.

On Yom Tov, Shimi stood like Moshe Rabbeinu blasting his ram's horn from the jagged mountaintop, only not a single disciple heeded his call. On Sukkot—Feast of the Tabernacles—he journeyed daily to the market square with his *lulav* and his *etrog*, a large, costly citrus nestled in palm fibers and encased in a silver egg. He tried to ignore the snickers. He tried to coax a few good-spirited townspeople into carrying out the mitzvah, but they brandished his branches at one another like court jesters at a duel.

He visited the local clergy. Why hadn't he thought of this before? Surely, the local Father would know where he could find relatives of the legendary 275. Have you tried the cemetery? the priest asked, closing his eyes and sprinkling him with myrrh. Shimi inhaled. The priest made the sign of the cross above Shimi's head.

• • •

HEADQUARTERS WAS NOT pleased. Krinsky tightened his purse strings. He stopped calling Shimi "son." Shimi pleaded his case. Anybody was better than nobody. Dutch sailors, French divorcees, a Cypriot dance troupe, all linking arms to the lyrics of Shalom Aleichem—was that not a beautiful *Yiddishkeit* sight? Couldn't we all use some peace in the heart? Wasn't this the

Lubavitcher mission? To spread light. To shrink the self in service to the divine. The smaller we are, the larger we are.

Winter tried his soul. The goat herd migrated to the valley. Elena stocked meals in the fridge. Braised rabbit soaked in red wine. Shimi did not have the heart to tell her that the animal was not kosher, so he tucked into his uneven table and voraciously ate, tears running down his face. It was delicious. He hungered to share it. From the cliff's edge, Shimi surveyed the abandoned beach where a lone rowboat was fastened by rope to the dock. It bobbed gently on the surface. Dmitri was nowhere to be found.

With little else to do, he struck out in search of the cemetery. It was hiding in plain sight, nestled along a steep slope of overgrowth behind a church not far from the town center. A Magen David was affixed to the wrought iron gate. There were many more graves than he would have thought, mottled with moss and sinking into the earth. The rows went on and on. As he walked among the dead, Shimi placed small memorial stones. He noted the dates. The oldest was from the 1600s. The most recent was from 1954. He sat beside it. The wind cut through him, raw and cold.

But spring signaled renewal, and summer sprang to life. The beach below turned topless. There was skin everywhere: un-self-conscious, unafraid. At first, Shimi looked away. Then he looked up from beneath his hat. Eventually, he stopped pretending not to look. Who could avert their eyes from such supple flesh—tattoos stretching flagrantly along the bronze length of a thigh? Rambam essentially agreed: the human body was a holy work of art. In his white shirt and black pants, Shimi stared. Occasionally, the sunbathers stared back.

One day he stumbled upon a rocky beach

near an old mining quarry. Men lazed around with their members hanging low between their legs. The sight stole his breath. The gathering of men in naked communion, like the baths at Brighton Beach with the invigorating *platzas* and the cups of cold borscht, filled him with joy. It gave him an idea. He printed flyers. *Men's Night! Shabbos Feast! All are welcome!* He slipped colored notices on car windshields, wedging them into the seats of scooters. There were so many beaches to cover. He stood over men who were lying like lizards in the sun, his shadow ruining their tanning long enough for them to extend a languid hand and take.

The tactic worked. Slowly, men came, like unfocused sea hatchlings emerging onto dry land. *Welcome! Come in!* Shimi subjected them to a quick Maariv service as soon as they numbered ten. Then he plied them with alcohol. Elena prepared the meal, plucking feathers in the yard all afternoon. He chanted. He sang. He blessed the bread and wine, he blessed the guests as if they were the children of Rachel, Leah, and Sarah, palming their warm heads, which made him long for the sweaty scalps of his own children careening down the halls of his in-laws and crashing into walls without anyone looking up from their prayer books to take notice.

Men's Night was a success. Not only was he offering home cooked food and wine—in addition to plenty of schnapps, ouzo, and raki—but he had beds to spare, too. For free! All he was asking in exchange was their presence, a little tolerance of Torah. This was *ben adam le chavero*. Men flocked. They were beautiful, long-limbed, well-traveled. They were flush with laughter and short on cash. He kept a pot of cholent simmering on the stove, light on the meat and heavy on the beans, for sustenance all weekend. They stood over it, spooning the warm stew into each other's mouths, wiping the errant dribble from their chins. Shimi beamed at the sight. The Ninth of Av was approaching, the saddest day of the year. If he couldn't make sense of senseless hatred, he could at least offer a small antidote to it.

Esti called on Sunday. They were moving, she said, leaving her crowded parents' house. Mazel tov, he said distractedly, lighting a cigarette, one onto the next, a recent habit. They rarely spoke by phone. Her voice, distilled of emotion, reached him as though through a long, dark tunnel. He couldn't listen. If she used the word settlement, he did not hear it.

And then—just like that—Dmitri was back. He raised a bottle by the neck like a trophy.

"Where have you been?" Shimi blurted.

"Here and there," Dmitri said. Shimi buried his hurt with a smile, and respected his friend's privacy. He was here now, and that's what mattered. Brightness had been restored to Dmitri's haunted eyes. They picked up where they'd left off. Maybe Shimi should have been embarrassed by how happy he felt, but Dmitri did not seem to mind. He did not try to quiet him. When you live in silence for so long, the sound of another becomes the unbidden harmony to the human heart. Dmitri never revealed details, never revealed the nature of his burden. Shimi drew assumptions on loss and distance. They smoked. They drank. Shimi's cheeks no longer broke into a novice rash from the licorice-flavored liquor. He'd grown used to it. He leaned against Dmitri's iron shoulder.

"I missed you, friend," he said. "It's been too long."

"What is time? Time is time."

They were sitting so close that their breathing fell into sync. For the very first time, Shimi did not feel alone in the world. His chest swelled with abundance. He squeezed his friend's hand, pumping it twice, then he smoothed the vein that bulged like an earthworm down its dorsal side. He was that grateful.

Men's Nights lasted all summer. Returning guests brought friends. Friends brought strangers. The steady flow of alcohol emboldened men to share their stories. Relying on English as a common denominator, they recounted hikes in Bulgaria, lake parties in Patagonia, the bathhouses of Japan, ayahuasca in Peru. Their journeys tunneled through Shimi's pores. In the rare conversational lull, he retold the story of the bishop and the mayor of Zakynthos, who stood up Spartacus-style, handing the Germans a sheet of paper with only their own names: "Here is your list of Jews."

Shimi raised his shot glass. "To life!"

"L'Chaim!" the men said. Out came another bottle. Shimi tried to teach them a song, and they banged on the table in rhythm. Sweaty shirts flew off, whipping overhead as the men pushed back from the table. Chairs found walls. Men began tousling on the ground in what looked like sport but could have been argument or affection. Like Jacob wrestling the angel, Shimi thought.

Later, in bed, his head still whirling, he listened to the echoes of laughter, to the primal joy, to the staccato spike of foreign tongues in adjacent rooms. They ignited his dreams, men in goat heads circling a bonfire, arms swaying high above the burning flames.

Dawn broke. A padded envelope arrived by post. It was from his eldest son Daniel, thanking him for the camera that Shimi had sent the boy for his birthday. Shimi flipped through photos: kids making clown faces, eating cake, doing a chicken dance. Shimi's favorites were the accidental ones: the swath of a fringed undershirt, a bare blurry foot. The off-centered haze of a night sky. He attached them by magnets to his fridge.

• • •

THAT FALL, Krinsky approved Shimi's request to visit his family. Upon landing in Tel Aviv, Shimi boarded a bus to Jerusalem. From there, he took a car to Gush Etzion. All he saw were green fatigues and evenly spaced loops of barbed wire. The driver grew quiet at the checkpoint. He rolled up their windows. Shimi was confused. Terracotta roofs blocked the horizon. He had the distinct feeling of trespassing, of being in a place where he was not only unwelcome but did not belong at all.

It was like walking onto the set of someone else's life. When he pushed open the front door, no one took notice. The children were sparring violently on the rug. Esti was cracking pomegranates on the counter, up to her wrists in the bloody, jewel-like meat.

“Say hello to your father,” Esti said, wiping her stained hands on a dish towel.

“Abba,” they said, from the crook of their armlocks.

“Children,” he said, kissing their heads, inhaling their scalps for a whiff of connection as they squirmed against his grip, eager to resume their activity.

His eldest, with hollow posture and pocked skin, stood dreamily apart. Daniel reminded Shimi of himself when he was that age. A Polaroid camera hung from a strap around his neck.

“Daniel,” he said. “Show me my room.”

The trip did not go as hoped. He’d never felt lonelier than while surrounded by his own family. The younger boys charged through the dusty hills all day long, pummeling Daniel with rubber band slingshots. They picked fruit off neighbors’ trees and threw it at each other, splitting the skins in waste. They were a cruel little gang. It gave Shimi *tsuris*.

"It is the will of G-d," Esti said.

Not my God, Shimi thought.

"Come home," he said soberly.

"I am home," Esti said with her back to him. Her elbows moved tightly as she punched down her dough. He stepped behind her, pushing aside the ends of her headscarf at the nape of her neck. As he touched her skin, she stiffened.

He tried again. "We can't have our children running amok."

"Tell that to Hashem."

He wanted to shake some sense into her. What she wanted was a *get*. To be released from legal union. There was an older rabbi from Cleveland whose wife had died. Cancer.

"A pity," Shimi said.

But what would headquarters say? A divorce

could cost Shimi his job. For this reason, he refused her a *get*. It was for her own good, he said. For their own good. Many families operated under similar pretenses. Esti cursed him with every Yiddish word for hypocrite, of which there were many.

...

HE WAS WHAT HE WAS, but what freedom would another marriage bring? For all intents and purposes, he said, she could go and do and live as she wished. Secrets were powerful things.

Meanwhile, back on Zante, a fresh crop of Chabadniks was awaiting the art of outreach. His outpost on the hill had acquired something of a reputation among misfits and outcasts. He'd heard of the Havasupai tribe who lived at the base of the Grand Canyon, born from ignominious exile. Other places shared similar origin stories: Australia, New Zealand. His Chabad had become New Zealand.

With fresh fervor, he welcomed these outliers. They were mixed-up and immature, nestled in the cloistered armpit of God for so long that they compulsively blinked at the light. They'd seen nothing, knew nothing of the outside world. They curved their shoulders like cats. They picked their skin. They twisted and twirled their sidelocks, rocking forward and backward on their thick-soled shoes. He found them playing with matches, he found them too close to the cliff, he found them toying with themselves, manipulating their members into origami shapes: a turtle, a seashell. He redirected their restless hands. He took away the matches, he steered them off the edge of the cliff. He talked to them as if they were his own children, with whom he rarely spoke anymore. If he was a negligent father, he could be a decent rabbi. What he could be was a human being.

Headquarters may have wanted Shimi to reform them so that they'd promptly return to the movement as law-abiding, eligible bachelors, but Shimi worried about tossing them back into the insular sea too soon, like discarding fish too meager to eat. The least he could do was teach them to swim. *Something*, he could teach them something.

He took them to the market, to the town square, to the beach. The boys blushed at the lithe figures rubbing each other in tanning oil. Remember, he said: shame did not exist in Gan Eden until the serpent arrived. So they watched shamelessly, like tourists on safari witnessing lions in heat.

He taught them to work. To tighten the pipes and patch the plaster and weed the stubborn herb garden. Calluses bloomed proudly on the idle pads of their fingers.

On Shabbos, they needed no encouragement to erupt into song. Wine sloshed in plastic cups as they pounded the table, chanting. They pounded until their fists chafed and reddened. Tears streaked their cheeks. The songs had no beginning and no end. They had no words, either, but it was the music that the boys knew by heart.

• • •

THEY WERE HAVING such a good time that many pupils were loath to leave. This presented a problem. Shimi had a limited curriculum. He could offer only so many chores. He could regurgitate choice passages from *Ethics of the Fathers* ("It is not your responsibility to finish the work, but neither are you free to desist from it") but his clumsy scholarship was better suited to the uninitiated. He could not sit around all day unpacking meaning. He had them dust the attic just to give them something to do. They discovered a small jewelry box containing one gold broach, a child's pair of lace-up shoes, and a stack of faded papers in Greek. He turned the findings over to Dmitri who held them out from his body like dead things.

What now?

"Goats," Dmitri proposed. They could count the goats. Monitor the goats. Milk the goats. Make cheese from the goats. They could learn the ritual of slaughter.

"Genius," Shimi said, clapping his friend on the back.

And so, a partnership emerged. It was like a trade school for wayward boys. They prayed, they packed lunches, they mingled among the lean, browsing animals, returning from their day's work with damp shirts. They could be reckless, these boys, but under Dmitri's tutelage the Chabadniks stopped hounding each other and learned to look after the herd. The animals regarded them with an indifference as old as time. A fresh goat head graced the fence post with each new moon.

As for Shimi, something inside him was shifting. An accrual of small things. When a student challenged a commandment, he no longer defended it by saying "because it is written." Law only went so far. Questions begat questions. He abandoned answers entirely. Whatever they were searching for could not be found in a book.

After Shavuot, while trimming his beard, his hand slipped, and a fuzzy hunk came off. The asymmetry was preposterous. Even Elena laughed. She lifted her shears. Shimi balked. No, he said. *Yes!* she insisted, in Greek, leading him to the generous kitchen sick. She massaged his temples, shampooed his scalp. He closed his eyes. A sigh escaped his lips. Afterward, he almost didn't recognize himself. His chin was as smooth as a baby's bottom.

On Purim, already half-blitzed, Dmitri took him to a nightclub, placed a little stamp on his tongue.

"Live a little," Dmitri said. "For me."

When had Dmitri ever asked anything of him?

It was there on the dance floor surrounded by painted strangers that Shimi felt the overwhelming presence of the universe's hidden saints. Amid a flash of sequin, a stretch of iridescence thin as a butterfly wing, were the *lamed vavniks*, the 36 unassuming individuals who were saving the world from ruin. The room softened and dissolved at its edges as he moved through the crowd. Light penetrated his being, radiated through his skin. Sweat poured from his brows. His arms were parabolic. The music pounded in sync with his own beating heart. Holiest of holies! There was no Mordechai or Haman, no good or evil. Rather, anyone could be anyone! Everyone was everyone! Could there be any greater joy?

Together their bodies forged a single, pulsing unit. He danced. Oh, how he danced! He raised his wrists. He jumped like a pogo stick. He swung partygoers from his elbows as if in a wedding circle. When he looked up, there was Dmitri, his head tilted back and his tongue out as if poised to catch fresh droplets of rain. What an angel! Shimi floated toward him only to be intercepted by a swarm of sirenic women. They removed his hat and slithered to his front and rear, pressing their heated curves into his sides, against his backside, into his member, the excitement building, until they swam away like a school of eels.

The removal of traditional garments came next. His *shtreimel* was a foolish extravagance, an accessory better suited to Russian winters than to the Greek island heat. The musty sable emitted such a pungent smell that he stored the hatbox in the closet and stopped taking it out, not even on the highest, holiest day. Was there a more spurious sight than the righteous in furs? And if he quit the suit jacket? Well, that was between him and Hashem. It, too, gave off a ripeness that did not serve him. He no longer swaddled himself in his heavy prayer shawl but allowed his breezy, fringed undergarments to suffice. He washed his shirts by hand and pinned them on the line, letting his bare shoulders freckle and burn in the sun. Never had he exposed himself like this. Still, he wore his yarmulke. It perfectly covered the burgeoning bald spot on his head.

Esti wrote: send money. He sent what he had. There was only so much. She wanted more. We all want things we can't have. Shimi thirsted for a plump, juicy orange in a skin so aromatic and thick it could be peeled in one strip, but the fruit did not grow in this region. Esti wanted to believe she was entitled to the fruit of her neighbors, that it was hers for the taking, but if Shimi believed in anything it was that land on this earth belonged to nobody.

One morning, a tour bus wheezed up the hill. Out spilled a blur of sunhats and lanyards and water bottles, the mid-Atlantic chapter of the Wandering Jews. Here on a 10-day Island-Hopping Pilgrimage, they'd been to Salonika, they'd visited the synagogue of Corfu. Rhodes was next on the itinerary after a brief stop in Zakynthos. The goats surrounded them. The goats were on the move. They bleated; they blocked the road. Tourists whipped out their phones as the pack of yeshiva *bochers* came running up behind them, shirttails flying. *What in God's name?!* Wandering Jews shouted as they confronted the stinking row of ruminant heads. Shimi assured them that the talismans were benign —to ward off the evil eye. Did they come in souvenir form? They wanted to know. Shimi shook his head. Selfies would have to suffice.

Of course, it only took one incident to turn the whole thing sideways. When Izzy Teitelbaum severed his thumb with a butcher knife, Krinsky put the kibosh on their enterprise. *What was Shimi thinking? Trusting these boys to slaughter?* Izzy Teitelbaum had a deranged look in his walleye. It could have been so much worse. He could have chopped off someone else's finger. Another appendage. *Halevai.* The Teitelbaums could sue. Krinsky couldn't abide this freewheeling survivor camp a minute longer, this twisted *Yiddishkeit* take on *Lord of the Flies*. Shimi Shem Tov protested. To the contrary, their hilltop experiment bred cooperation, equanimity, and kindness. Krinsky tsked. "It's only a matter of time until people turn against each other." Shimi should stay away from goats. Stick to what he knows.

What did he know? Shimi chewed his cuticles until they bled onto the Talmud, dotting the text with blood, as the words of Rabbi Hillel leapt out like a riddle before him. "If I am not for me, who will be for me? And when I am for myself alone, what am I? And if not now, then when?" The words felt like a trap.

The unfortunate matter of Izzy Teitelbaum put a strain on his friendship with Dmitri. Dmitri resented the unwanted attention, the legal threats, the flurry of taxis and commotion, as the young men summarily packed up and left.

Before Shimi could come up with anything to make it up to him, Dmitri pushed off in his little boat. Shimi was alone again with his warring desires. Once Dmitri had said something about men being islands, but it struck Shimi as false. As if the words hadn't come from him. Dmitri had also said, "Goats go down the hill. Goats go up the hill." That was more like it.

With his fall from grace came liberation. Shimi Shem Tov was free of Krinsky, free of group pressure, free of expectation. Finally, he could think for himself. He roamed the sparse hills. What did he think? Fresh air was good to breathe. People were unknowable. If Esti wanted a *get*, he'd give her the *get*. What was he holding onto? In return, he wrote: *please send the children.*

Daniel came. His eldest arrived with a rainbow swirled yarmulke on his head and his whole life in a nylon frame pack. Shimi nearly burst. "It's you! My boy!" He clutched him to his chest. "You made it!" His son had refused army service, would not fight for what he did not believe, so he was traveling. He was a lank rattle of bones. How many years had it been? There were holes in his ears, a ring in his nose. A loose scarf garnished his neck. His hair was as long as it had been before his first *upsherin.* "Stay as long as you like!" Shimi said. He showed him the goats. Daniel was more interested in the sea. Down they went to the sea, shedding their clothes like they were on fire. They ran right in.

In all his life, Shimi had never done this before. Of all the rituals! He felt invigorated! Alive!

Afterward, Dmitri was waiting in his pickup to bring them to town.

"This is Daniel!" Shimi said, proudly. "My son."

"Hop in," Dmitri said.

They squeezed three abreast in the cab. Shimi felt giddy. They drove to the square, sat at an outdoor café. Strangers nodded in recognition. By now, the last rabbi of Zakynthos was an island fixture. He lit a cigarette. Daniel took out his pouch of tobacco and finger-length sheaths of paper and adeptly rolled his own. "Like father, like son!" Dmitri said. They drank Mythos straight from green bottles. Daniel had been to Ecuador, to Cambodia, to Laos. He called no place home. His reports reminded Shimi of the Men's Night stories from long ago.

"What have you found in all this searching and seeking and bouncing around?"

Daniel shrugged.

They drank until they were red and sweaty and hungry. In the morning, Daniel was gone. He left a note. There was a party in Mykonos. He'd been only passing through.

• • •

THAT WAS FIVE YEARS ago already. Since then, Elena died. Dmitri buried her. He posted no goat heads during this period, their carcasses stewing until they slipped off the wire and dissolved into a pool of decay. From dust to dust. For thirty days, Shimi recited the mourner's prayer three times a day as if Elena were his own mother. He had not heard from his own parents for some time: his parents who'd traded their VW van for a Honda Odyssey, who lived in the tight breast of community, who first taught him the mantra "God will provide." What would they have done, he often wondered, if a strange family in need came to their door? He knew what the Torah teaches. But living by it was something else. When push came to shove, would they have let in the dispossessed?

The last time he went into town, graffiti desecrated his posters. There were penises and swastikas galore. This was hardly a shock. For years, no one had been coming to his Learning Luncheons, to his Men's Nights, to his Move and Meditate retreats.

And now a sickness of Biblical proportion was spreading. Everyone had been ordered to stay indoors, as if the plague might pass over them.

Never did he expect it would come for Dmitri. Invincible Dimitri.

The goat herder, his dear friend, a man of few words, had not even mentioned in recent weeks that he'd been sick. Days passed before Shimi pieced it together, the goats signaling their grief in desperate plea.

By the time Shimi ventured into Dmitri's home, Dmitri's body had begun to turn. The scent of neglect unmoored him. There was no *chevra kadisha*, no one to watch over the soul of his friend who'd faithfully watched over him in this foreign country for all these years.

With Dmitri's death, Shimi was bereft. He broke down and wept. When he regained himself, he decided: he would prepare the burial himself.

It was in the ritual washing, the scrubbing of ears, the painstaking scraping beneath the fingernails, that Shimi finally beheld Dmitri's circumcision. He paused at the sight, Dmitri's manhood no bigger than a field mouse in from the cold. As at each of his sons' *brit milah*, Shimi felt called to seal the covenant with his lips. Instead, he carefully wrapped the body in a simple shroud and dug into the family plot on the hill. That's when he noticed several other mounds, unmarked and indistinguishable. How many people had once dotted these hills? Who wasn't a lost Jew of Zakynthos? There were so many things Shimi would never know. This much he knew: his time on the island was done.

• • •

OF COURSE, he's always known this day would come. All things come to an end. Here he was, at 42, at the ragged edge of this remote earth wracked by a crisis of faith. He does not know what to do or where to go. Brooklyn feels like another planet. Who will mind the herd?

He shuts the makeshift wire gate, shuffling along the narrow dirt road toward the bluff. There is a pebble in his shoe, but he doesn't bother to remove it. Below, waves smash into boulders. The beach is deserted. Western winds blow off his sad, black hat.

Today the animals are hiding, as if they do not wish to face their fate. Vertigo grips him as he peers over the edge, and he stumbles backward to regain his footing. As the sun slides like a large yolk into the horizon, Shimi Shem Tov removes his wool coat. He rolls up his sleeves. A swim, he decides. He'll go for a fortifying swim.

Slowly, he begins to disrobe. Shoes, socks, slacks. He unbuttons and discards his white shirt. He is standing there in his *tzitzit* and briefs when he hears the rumble of tires on the unpaved road, the crunch of dirt, an echo of his own arrival all those years ago.

A young woman climbs out of the taxi. She wears a mauve peasant blouse and a long skirt. A mask covers her nose, mouth, and chin. The driver gets out, heaving his passenger's suitcases out of the trunk. There is a mask on his face, too. Money changes hands. In nothing but his undergarments, Shimi watches the long-haired figure. There is something so familiar in her body language, her willowy gestures. She reminds him of himself.

"Abba," she cries, waving tentatively.

Tears wet his face. It's been so long since anyone called him that. Even from this distance he recognizes the person standing before him as his first born. The child who made him a father.

"It's me, Dani."

"I've been waiting for you." Shimi opens his arms, and she runs into them.

BIO

Sara Lippmann loves a good story.